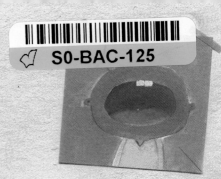

S0-BAC-125

To:

_____

From:

_____

Date:

_____

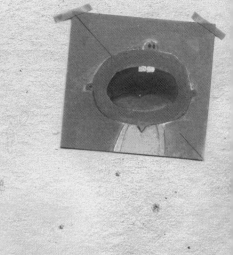

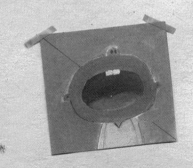

The Splatters
Learn Some Manners

Marty Mokler Banks
Illustrated by Cecilia Rébora

HARVEST HOUSE PUBLISHERS
EUGENE, OREGON

To my parents,
Jerry and Lloyd Mokler. MMB

To Mateo and the little one for
all the happiness. Cecilia Rébora

The Splatters Learn Some Manners

Text Copyright © 2009 by Marty Mokler Banks
Art Copyright © 2009 by Cecilia Rébora

Published by Harvest House Publishers
Eugene, Oregon 97402
www.harvesthousepublishers.com

ISBN: 978-0-7369-2558-7

Original illustrations by Cecilia Rébora. Regarding the art in this book, you may contact
Cecilia at MB Artists, 10 East 29th Street, #40G, New York, NY 10016, 212-689-7830

Design and production by Mary pat Design, Westport, Connecticut

All rights reserved. No part of this publication may be reproduced, stored in a retrieval
system, or transmitted in any form or by any means—electronic, mechanical, digital,
photocopy, recording, or any other—except for brief quotations in printed reviews,
without the prior permission of the publishers.

Printed in Singapore

09 10 11 12 13 14 15 / IM / 10 9 8 7 6 5 4 3 2 1

Manners are crazy things. Different cultures have different manners, and even in Western culture manners can mean very different things from one family to the next.

So how are kids supposed to learn basic manners?
As parents, we try and teach them. But then our lives get busy, or it becomes too tiring to repeat the same direction, or we just simply forget good manners ourselves. Or we're really firm about manners, but sometimes our kids forget.
Raising kids is hard work, and nobody's perfect.

This book is intended to be a fun romp rather than a severe lesson. I hope kids are drawn to the Splatters because of the wacky, rhythmic language and the colorful, lively illustrations.
I hope kids love the story so much it becomes a favorite childhood book. And along the way, who knows?
They might even learn a manner...or two!

Marty Mokler Banks

The Splatters are messy,
Disheveled, uncouth.
So vulgar and sloppy,
It's just the sad truth!

Dad Egbert spills soup on
The dog's lumpy coat.
Son Rupert drips glue on
The homework he wrote.

Sly Lumpert is pesky
And teases young Ted.
Tot Molly's cling peaches
Drip down her blonde head.

Tall Filbert rolls dishes
For Digbert to chase,
While blobs of burnt oatmeal
Spot Grandmother's lace.

The paints are uncovered,
The beds left undone,

8

The chairs lie tipped sideways,
The trash weighs a ton.

So one day the Duchess
Delivers a note
That's topped with gold glitter,
And here's what she wrote:

"You Splatters, my subjects,
I hear it is told
Your children run wild,
Your house smells of mold.

11

"So here is my edict
To be done today.
You'll join me for supper
At Fancy Café!

"But first you must clean house,
Then dress in your best.
I'll not have my subjects
An item of jest."

The Splatters were cheerful.
They squealed in delight.

A whoop-de-do dinner
As soon as tonight!

But Mother waxed anxious
With chores still to do.
She sat her clan down for
A real talking-to.

"We've been a bit lazy,
We've been a smidge lax,
But now it is time to
Adjust to the facts.

"We'll clean and we'll vacuum
From ceiling to floor.
We'll scrub with our muscles
Until they are sore."

NEWS

The children all toiled
And grumbled to boot,
But soon they were free of
All messes and soot.

"So perfect, my darlings,"
Mom crowed to her crew.
"And now we must learn a
Quick manner or two."

GOOD MANNERS

"When sitting for dinner,
First take off your cap.
Then place the cloth napkin
Down flat on your lap.

"No fishing for ice cubes,
No tag with the chairs.
No screeching or screaming,
No flinging éclairs.

"Wipe smears off your chin and
Use spoon, knife, and fork.
Then chew with your mouth shut
When eating your pork.

"Don't dangle long noodles,
Don't lob your green peas.
And always make sure to
Say 'Thank you' and 'Please.'"

The Splatters were gracious
When Duchess arrived

To find the house gleaming
And spotless inside.

27

So off to her limo
The group trooped along.
Then sped to the Café
While trilling a song.

Upon their arrival
They walked in so proud.
Then sat still for dinner
As Duchess was wowed.

29

"I find you so polished,
I give you such praise.
It's time to bestow my
Rare Duchess Parfaits."

Mom Splatter groaned low at
The sweets so supreme.
"Oh dear, did I mention
The rules for... whipped cream?"

I seek constantly to improve
my manners and graces,
for they are the *sugar*
to which all are attracted.

Og Mandino

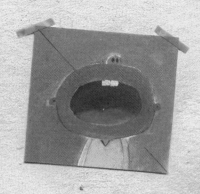

Please!

Thank You!

Please!

Thank You!

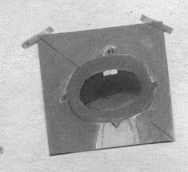